THE HAUN

RENEGADE X

CHELSEA M. CAMPBELL

1st edition published by Golden City Publishing, 2016

Cover art by Chloë Tisdale.

ISBN: 0-9898807-7-X
ISBN-13: 978-0-9898807-7-0

Books by Chelsea M. Campbell

Renegade X
The Rise of Renegade X
The Trials of Renegade X
The Haunting of Renegade X
The Betrayal of Renegade X

Fire & Chasm
Starlight
Growing Up Dead
Harper Madigan: Junior High Private Eye

DEDICATION

For everyone who loves these characters as much as I do.

THE HAUNTING OF RENEGADE X

CHAPTER 1

"Who has a Halloween party the day before Halloween?" I ask Kat. We're walking downtown, on our way to her dad's office party. A party that Kat's parents insisted she go to—since she's doing so well at Vilmore and, like, going places or whatever—and that they specifically banned me from. Her dad actually banned me from all company events, after the incident at Homecoming a few weeks ago, but he went out of his way to remind her not to bring me to this one.

"Lots of people," Kat says. It's cold out—the kind of cold that makes your nose hurt—and she pulls her coat tighter around her against a sharp gust of wind. "And my dad's having the party tonight so his employees can take their kids trick-or-treating tomorrow."

"Or go to their friends' parties."

Kat scowls at that. "You should come over."

I raise my eyebrows at her, because it's not exactly the warmest invitation, what with her sort of glaring at me. "I

1

thought you had a test in the morning." It's the reason why she has to go back to school tonight, and why her parents are driving her back there as soon as the party's over. I doubt they'd be very happy about bringing me with them, but I could always take the train and meet her at her dorm.

"I meant you should come over *tomorrow* night. We could still spend Halloween together."

I let out a deep breath. I don't really know Kat's friends —though I do know they all call her Katie and that it still weirds me out—and I kind of doubt that "spending Halloween together" would be just us. And the idea of going all the way over to her dorm, just so I can watch her share in-jokes with a bunch of people I don't know, and then having to scramble to get back in time for school in the morning, doesn't exactly sound that appealing. Besides, as much as I'd like to spend the night with her anyway—in spite of how little I might fit in with her friends and her new life at school—I have plans. "I'm going to Sarah's tomorrow." Something she already knows, which is why she was scowling at me.

Kat sort of disapproves of my friendship with Sarah. Maybe more like *a lot* disapproves. Especially after Sarah went temporarily insane and tried to kill me.

"You could come, too," I tell her. "If you want."

Kat gives me this horrified look, as if I just asked her to go kick puppies with me or something. "That's the last thing that I—" She stops walking—so suddenly that someone behind us almost runs into her—and wraps her arms around herself. When she speaks again, she keeps her

2

voice low. "Come on, Damien. Let's cross the street."

"Why? Is there—" I think at first that she's avoiding someone, but before I can offer to zap them for her, I look up and see the Golden City Banking and Finances building. A shiver runs up my spine. "*Oh.*"

"I haven't been back here since, you know, that thing with Pete."

She means when my ex-best friend Pete took her captive, tied her up on the roof, and tried to force me to torture her. Calling it "that thing with Pete" is putting it lightly, and I can see why she hasn't been back. Why neither of us have. I swallow. "It's just a building."

Just my least favorite building in the whole world, possibly the universe. Because not only was Kat held hostage there, but I went plummeting to my death from the top of the ridiculously high roof. *Twice.* To say I don't like heights would be an understatement, but the one thing I hate even more than heights is falling from them.

She steps on a leaf on the pavement, flattening it with a *crunch.* "I know it's stupid, but it creeps me out."

"It's not stupid. If it was up to me, this thing would have been demolished months ago."

"So let's cross the street." She takes my hand.

I don't move. "I might really hate this building, Kat, but crossing the street to get away from it feels like... I don't know, like letting it win. Besides, it wasn't the building's fault all that stuff happened. It was Pete."

"Still," Kat says.

"Pete was the problem, and he's dead. So, there's nothing to be afraid of." Just some horrible, traumatizing

3

memories is all.

Kat looks up at the building, then back at me again, seeming pretty unconvinced. But then she sighs and says, "Okay, fine. We'll walk past it. But if it, like, collapses on top of us or something, I'm blaming you. And don't think I won't be able to blame you if I'm dead, because I'll totally haunt you."

"Won't I be dead, too, in this scenario?"

"You think ghosts can't haunt other ghosts?" She rolls her eyes at me, then hurries forward as the *walk* light turns green.

When we get to the Banking and Finances building, we both look up. My stomach drops as I relive falling from the top of this thing, and I kind of maybe wish I'd listened to her and just crossed the street.

Beside me, Kat shudders. "Come on," she says, speeding up. "I want to spend as little time here as possible."

"Go ahead. I'll catch up in a minute."

She looks at me like I'm crazy, then shrugs and walks off, like she can't get past this thing fast enough. I don't blame her, and part of me wonders why I'm not doing the same thing. But if I can't even stand here and look at this place, then it doesn't just feel like *it's* winning—it feels like *Pete's* winning.

And okay, maybe looking up at the roof made me want to throw up, and that's probably never going to change. But here? It's just the front of a building. Er, well, some bad stuff went down here, too, but not nearly as bad as what happened on the roof. This is a place of business. There are big glass doors, and I can see people sitting at their desks, typing away at their computers and answering phone calls. Someone in a suit comes out, carrying a briefcase. He holds the door open and gives a me a questioning look, but I shake my head, and he lets it go.

Standing outside and facing it is one thing, but there's no way I'm going inside.

Kat's waiting for me at the end of the block, picking up her feet and rubbing her arms in the cold.

I turn to go.

And that's when I hear Pete's voice. *Hey, Damien. Been waiting for you, man—long time no see.*

I freeze. The voice sounds tinny, like it's being broadcast through an old speaker. I glance around, my heart racing, even though...

Even though Pete's *dead*, and there's no way I just heard that.

There's an ATM next to the front doors. It must have made a noise or something. Something that sounded like my ex-best friend who's been dead for six months. My ex-best friend whose superpower was being able to broadcast signals, like to a radio or a TV. Or maybe even an ATM.

My blood turns cold, and the hair on my arms stands up. Little sparks of lightning run along my back.

Kat's watching me, her eyebrows raised.

I hurry to catch up with her. "Did you hear that?" I ask.

"Hear what? Are you okay? Because you look kind of... not."

"I'm fine. I was just..."

I was just thinking about Pete and then imagined I heard him talking to me in the same place where he died. But that's all. No big deal.

"I thought someone said my name. But I guess I was wrong."

CHAPTER 2

"**W**ell?" Amelia says. "What do you think?" She means the dress she's wearing. It's Halloween night, and with the rest of the family out trick-or-treating, I guess she didn't have anyone else to ask.

"I think I'm busy," I tell her, not looking away from the TV screen, since me and Riley are in the middle of a particularly intense round of *Villains vs. Heroes*. We're mostly killing time until we go over to Sarah's for her party, but that doesn't mean it's not important that I kick his ass.

"Can't you pause?" Amelia asks, even though she knows about my strict no-pause policy. "I just need you to look over here for a second. I have to leave soon."

Riley glances over at her, then back at the screen. "You look fine."

Amelia lets out a squeak of outrage. "*Fine?!*"

"Um." Riley looks back and forth between her and the game. "I just meant Zach won't care what you look like."

She gasps, then stomps in front of the TV.

Now he's done it.

"Hey!" I lean to the side, trying to see around her, though it's kind of pointless now, since Riley just lost.

"Damien, you have to tell me the truth." She gestures to the dress, which is bright purple and has puffy sleeves and frilly ruffles around the waist, like the designer thought what the skirt really needed was a tutu shoved on top of it.

"Great job," I tell her. "Scariest costume ever. You might as well clear a space for the trophy right now."

She glares at me. "It's not supposed to be scary! And it's not a costume." She fidgets, tugging at the edges of her poofy sleeves. "I borrowed this from Tiffany. It's her best dress."

"Seriously? Is it also, maybe, her *only* dress?"

Amelia folds her arms. "Well, maybe it's not her *best* one, but it was the only one that fit me. She had to wear it to a wedding last year. She was a bridesmaid."

"I think that went without saying."

"I *can't* wear my pink one again." She sighs and flops down on the couch between us, her dress making a lot of rustling noises. "I always wear it, and Zach's already seen me in it a couple times."

"So?" Riley asks, setting his controller on the coffee table.

"So, everyone will know that I only have the one dress because nothing else looks good on me."

I raise my eyebrows at her. "And you think *that's* going to change their minds?"

8

"Why did both Mom and Dad have to take Alex and Jess trick-or-treating? If Mom was here..." Amelia looks herself over and doesn't finish that sentence, presumably because it's obvious even Helen would have a hard time convincing her to wear that in public.

"It's not too late to put some zombie makeup on and tell everyone you were going for 'terrifying' on purpose."

She glances at the clock. "I'm supposed to meet Zach in ten minutes. I don't have time to put on extra makeup or to change clothes."

"I think," Riley says slowly, choosing his words carefully this time, "that Zach would understand being a couple minutes late. If you wanted to change first."

Amelia gapes at him. "I thought you said he wouldn't care!"

"He won't!" Riley holds up his hands in defeat. "He probably won't mind waiting for you, either. That's all."

She gives him a skeptical look, kicking one leg against the couch.

"You know, Amelia," I tell her, "you're right. You really don't have time to change. Boys like girls who are punctual. And to make sure you get there on time, Perkins here will even give you a ride."

"I will?" He wrinkles his eyebrows. "I mean, of course I will. It's getting dark out, and it's not like we're really doing anything."

"Well, *some* of us are losing at *Villains vs. Heroes*."

"I got distracted. That's all."

"Uh-huh. So it's settled. Amelia stays in that dress, and you drive us over to your house."

"Someone's got to stay here and hand out candy," Amelia says. "That's you."

"Yeah, I don't think so. I have a party to go to tonight, too, remember? And, anyway, there's no way I'm missing Zach's face when he sees you like that."

<h2 style="text-align:center">X·X·X</h2>

"Oh. My. God," Amelia says when we get to Riley and Zach's house. "What *is* that?"

Zach's standing in the doorway. He's got some kind of half alien, half octopus costume on, complete with extra tentacles hanging at his sides. His face is covered in silver and blue face paint, and his hair—which is caked in silver hairspray to match his face—is sticking straight up.

"It's my costume." Zach says that like it's super obvious, which it is.

"Oh. My. God."

"I'm Brogdon? The Third? You know, from Alien Star Raiders?" Zach's voice gets more high-pitched the more questions he asks and the more Amelia just stares at him like they've never met before. "It's my favorite video game. Well, my favorite *online* game, I mean."

"Maybe we should go inside," Riley says. "It's cold out."

I can't tell if he's saying that because we can see our breath, or if he just doesn't want Amelia making a scene in possible view of the neighbors, not to mention any trick-or-treaters.

Zach doesn't move—he's understandably too busy

10

watching Amelia for signs of stroke or aneurysm, since her brain seems to have shorted out—but Riley pushes past him into the house. Me and Amelia follow him, so I guess her brain must be working at least a little bit.

As soon as the door's closed, she glares at Zach. "I can't believe you!"

"What?" He glances down at himself, then at her. "You said it was a costume party."

"No, I said we had to *dress up*."

"Right. In costumes."

"*Dress up* means you're supposed to dress *nice*. Like, formal wear?"

"Oh." Zach blinks, taking that in. Then his eyebrows come together. "But if it's not a costume party, why are you wearing that?"

Amelia's face turns red. "It's not a costume!" She shoots me and Riley an accusing look, as if this is somehow our fault. She holds out her hand and uses her superpower to call up her pink dress, teleporting it from home. "I'm going to get changed. When I'm done, you'd better be dressed *up*. As in, *not* dressed as an alien."

"What? But I spent hours on this!" Zach's mouth hangs open a little, and he glances over at us, silently begging for help. "I printed out a picture to make sure I got my face just right!"

"Too bad. You should have thought of that before you misunderstood what *dress up* means."

"Okay, I... I guess I can..." Zach glances at his phone. "We're going to be late, though. And I'll have to shower, unless you think I can leave my hair like this."

Amelia wrinkles her nose at him. "No way. And shower fast. We're leaving in *ten minutes.*"

"Yeah. Okay. But—"

She takes her dress and disappears into the bathroom, shutting the door in Zach's face.

"But how am I supposed to shower if you're in there?"

"Use the one in Mom's room," Riley says.

"Or," I add, "you could, I don't know, *not* throw away hours of face-paint work? Take a stand. Don't be that guy who lets his girlfriend change him."

"I can hear you!" Amelia shouts, her voice muffled by the bathroom door.

"If you really cared about him, you'd want what's best for Zach!" I shout back.

"What's best for Zach is making his girlfriend happy! He'd better be getting in the shower right now if he knows what's good for him!"

Zach swallows. "Sorry, Damien. I have to go." He hurries off to their mom's room to do Amelia's bidding.

Riley's phone chimes at almost the same time as mine. We both look at our screens. It's a text from Sarah that reads, *Running late. Don't be here until 7:15. I'll keep you posted. I love you.*

Another text immediately follows: *Oops, forgot I was texting both of you. That last part was meant for Riley.*

Followed by another: *Not that I don't love you, too, Damien, but only as a friend.*

And one more: *Okay, signing off. This party isn't going to set up itself.*

Maybe not, but it would probably go a lot faster if she'd

let us help. But when we offered—well, when Riley offered; technically all I said was that I'd be happy to eat some of the cupcakes, so she didn't have as many to worry about—Sarah said she didn't want anyone coming over until she was done setting up. She also said she'd have everything ready by six thirty, but I guess it's taking her longer than she thought.

It's only a little after five, which means we have two hours left to kill.

Riley turns on the TV, and we both flop down on the couch.

"You want to watch a movie or something?" he asks, slowly flipping through the channels. "There are all these Halloween ones on, and— Oh! This one's great. Have you seen it?"

There's a man in a business suit running through a dark alley. He keeps looking over his shoulder at whatever's chasing him and then almost stumbling as he runs for his life.

"It's called *I Know How You Killed Me*. It's kind of cheesy, but me and Zach watch it every year. It's about this guy who's haunted by his dead best friend."

"Sounds boring." And not like what happened to me yesterday. Not at all.

"It's actually his dead *ex*-best friend. They had a falling out before he died, and the main guy sort of killed him, and his ex-best friend's ghost is out for revenge, but they don't know that really what happened is— Well, I don't want to spoil it. And it's not boring."

"Let's watch something else." Not that I'm freaked out

13

by the similarities between this stupid movie and what happened to me. I mean, what I *think* happened to me. Except I don't even think that that happened to me because I *know* there's no way I actually heard Pete's voice. It's impossible. And I'm not freaked out by it, or by this movie. It's just obviously stupid is all.

"What? No way. I know it's campy and the special effects are ridiculous, because it's from the 80s, but I swear you'll like it. Just give it a chance, X."

Now the guy on the screen has fallen down into a pile of trash in the alley, and there are a bunch of flashing lights that I think are supposed to be the ghost. The guy's screaming at it and begging it not to hurt him. And it *is* super cheesy, like Riley said, and there's absolutely no reason to be afraid of it, since I'm not, like, five years old. But it's also making me think of Pete, which wasn't exactly my favorite subject *before* what, um, didn't happen yesterday, and the last thing I want is to spend the next hour and a half—probably more like two hours, with commercials—thinking about my own dead ex-best friend. And whether or not he's trying to haunt me, which he isn't.

"I'm your guest," I tell Riley. "And the guest always chooses the movie."

He wrinkles his eyebrows. "Since when? And why can't you just trust me for once and try it out? This is, like, my favorite Halloween movie."

The bathroom door opens, and Amelia comes out, a little red in the face but successfully changed into her pink dress. "That's better," she says, smoothing down her hair with her hands. "Where's Zach?"

"Uh, it's been, like, two minutes," I remind her. "It's going to take him at least three to scrub all that face paint off."

"Zach!" she shouts in the direction of his mom's room. "You'd better hurry up!" Then she leans against the back of the couch and peers at the TV. "Oh! I love this movie."

Riley gives me a pointed look. "See? It's great."

"Yeah, I don't think Amelia liking it proves your point."

"Hey!" she whines.

"She's a guest," Riley says.

"But she's not *your* guest. And she's only going to be here for a few more minutes."

He stares at me for a second, like he can't figure out why I'm being like this. "It's a good movie. I'm not changing it."

"Some host you are." But I'm thinking maybe it won't be so bad. Maybe if I actually pay attention, I'll get so involved in the story that I won't be thinking about Pete, anyway.

Then a commercial comes on. It's for one of the businesses in the Golden City Banking and Finances building, and there's a shot of the outside of it. A shiver runs up my spine, and a sick feeling settles in my stomach.

"You know what? Let's not even watch TV." I make a grab for the remote. "We could play a game."

Riley jerks it away. "We played a game at your house."

"We played *Villains vs. Heroes*. I haven't kicked your ass at *Aliens vs. Dinosaurs IV* yet."

He scowls at me. "What the hell is wrong with you?"

15

"*Nothing.* A better question is, what the hell is wrong with *you*? You're the one forcing me to watch this."

Amelia gasps and puts a hand to her mouth. "Wait."

No. No, no, no. "You know what, Amelia? I think I hear Zach getting out of the shower. You should probably get ready to leave. As in, go stand out on the porch."

"Didn't *you* have a friend that died?"

"What?" Riley says, all the anger suddenly draining out of him.

"And didn't you kill him?"

"What?! *No.*" I glare at her. "I didn't kill anybody. And he wasn't my friend. Not... not by then."

They're both staring at me.

The movie comes back on. Riley holds up the remote and turns off the TV.

Now would be a great time for my phone to ring. Or for the house to catch on fire.

"I didn't know, X," Riley says, all sincere and apologetic. Which I know I should be grateful for, but instead all I feel is resentful. He's being a good friend, and all I can think about is how much I don't want to be talking about this. Or for him to know about it. Either of them, really.

"You could have just told me," he adds. Not like he's blaming me or anything. More like he really means it.

I shrug and don't look at him. "There's nothing to tell."

Amelia snorts. "Yeah, right."

"Don't you have somewhere to be? Like, laying out Zach's clothes for him or something?"

"*No.* Zach doesn't need me to..." She hesitates,

obviously tempted, but then resists. "I'm not missing this. You never told me what happened. Not really. I want to know how Keith died."

"Pete! His name was *Pete*. But it was a long time ago—"

"Uh, like, six months ago?"

"—and it doesn't matter now!"

Riley's looking at me like he knows that's not true. Like it not being true is the most obvious thing in the world.

"Look, he was my ex-best friend."

"Just like in the movie," Amelia says.

"Uh-huh. Shouldn't you go call whoever's throwing the party and tell them you're going to be late?"

"It's casual."

"But you had to put on a dress and make Zach change out of his costume? It doesn't sound casual. It sounds like the kind of party it would be really rude to be late for. Especially without even calling."

"I'm not leaving. I want to hear this."

"There's nothing to hear. And what if there are door prizes? Like, for cutest couple?"

"Cutest couple?" Her ears perk up at that.

"This could be your chance. But, as late as you're going to be, they'll probably assume you're not coming and give the award to someone else. Oh, well."

"You think we have a chance at cutest couple?"

"Well, Zach's pretty cute. And showing him off to all your friends is kind of the point of going to this party. Winning an award for it is something you can treasure for the rest of your life. But just knowing you're the cutest couple is its own reward, right? You don't *need* anything to prove it. And if some other couple gets the award, and everyone spends the whole night telling them how cute they are, well, that won't bother you, right?"

"Um."

"Because you'll know the truth. Deep down inside."

"I'm just going to go make a quick phone call. *Don't* tell the story until I get back." She points at me, then hurries into the kitchen to use the landline. Because, unlike everyone else in the world, Amelia doesn't have a cell phone.

A tiny part of me hopes that after all that, Riley will just forget what we were talking about and go back to watching TV, even though he already turned it off. But of course that doesn't happen.

"He was your ex-best friend?" Riley says, not even forgetting where I was in my explanation.

"Emphasis on the *ex* part. We hadn't been friends for a whole year before it happened. I mean, we were more like enemies. He tried to kill me. It wasn't like what happened with your dad." Riley and Zach's dad died a few years ago during a bus bombing. He sacrificed himself to save a lot of people. A decision that, understandably, Riley's still not okay with. But that was his *dad*. Someone he actually liked. This was different.

Riley's shaking his head. "Grief doesn't work that way. You can't put rules on it."

"I'm not grieving." I just don't want to think about Pete or what happened when he died or what for sure didn't happen yesterday.

He tilts his head, giving me a skeptical look.

"I'm not. I hadn't really even been thinking about Pete until..."

"Until the movie? I'm your friend, X. You could have just told me. I would have understood. I *do*, I mean."

"No. It's not that." And no matter how much he thinks he understands, will he still feel that way when I tell him I heard Pete talking to me and am apparently insane? "This is going to sound stupid, but I—"

A shriek from the kitchen interrupts me. "Oh, no," Amelia wails, running into the living room. "I just talked to Kim."

"And she got those photos of you in the bridesmaid dress I sent her, and you're automatically disqualified for cutest couple?" I ask.

"That's not true. I know you didn't take pictures of me, because you didn't even have your phone out. You were too busy playing video games. And you don't even have Kim's number."

"I was joking. Obviously."

"Well, don't! This is serious!"

"What's serious?" Zach asks, coming out of his mom's room. His hair's wet—and no longer silver—and he has a towel around his waist.

"It's a costume party!"

He stops moving and blinks at her. "What?"

Amelia covers her face with her hands. "According to Kim, *dress up* meant *costume party*. We're supposed to be wearing costumes! And there's even prizes for the best ones."

Zach's mouth falls open. A strangled croak escapes his

throat. "But… But I spent hours…"

"I know," Amelia squeaks, still hiding her face.

Riley rolls his eyes at them. "Come on," he says, jerking his head toward his room and getting up from the couch.

I follow him. Once we're inside, he shuts the door, muffling the sounds of Amelia and Zach's costume drama.

He sits down in his computer chair. "You want to tell me what's going on? I mean, you don't have to. If you don't want to talk about it, but—"

"I heard a ghost yesterday."

"You…" His forehead wrinkles up. "You saw a ghost?"

"No, I *heard* a ghost. I was at the Golden City Banking and Finances building—me and Kat were—and I swear I heard Pete's voice coming from an ATM."

There's a long pause. Then Riley just says, "Oh."

"I'm not crazy, Perkins." I pace back and forth in front of his bed. "Pete could broadcast signals. It was his superpower. And that was where he died. I hadn't been back since. Neither had Kat."

"And she heard it, too?"

"No. She wasn't close enough. And I know how that sounds—how all of it sounds—but *something* happened."

"Huh."

"Don't give me that."

"Don't give you what?"

"You can't just say *huh*, like you think this is interesting. Like you don't think I'm crazy."

"Well, I don't."

"But you probably *should*. And for the record, I don't believe in ghosts."

"Neither do I."

"Great. So which is it? You don't believe in ghosts, or you don't think I'm crazy? Because I don't see how it can be both."

"We should go down there. To the Golden City Banking and Finances building."

I stop pacing. "Seriously?"

"We've still got two hours before we can go over to Sarah's."

"So you want to go ghost hunting? On Halloween?"

He grins. "What better time for it? And anyway, we're not ghost hunting. But whatever happened there is obviously bothering you, whether it was what happened yesterday or six months ago."

"It was seven months. Not that I'm counting."

"Until you figure out what you heard, and why, you're not going to be able to let it go. We might as well check it out."

I consider that. "You're the only person I've told about this. Not even Kat knows. And I don't want her to." It would just freak her out.

"I won't tell anyone, X."

"Okay." I let out a deep breath. A part of me is actually relieved that we're going to go down there. Because he's right—I won't be able to let go until I know what the hell's going on. And if I imagined the whole thing because it turns out I'm not over my ex-best friend trying to kill me and then falling to his death, at least I'll know.

"Okay," I say again, nodding this time. "Let's do this."

CHAPTER 3

"This is it?" Riley asks, frowning at the ATM in front of the Banking and Finances building.

"I don't know what you were expecting, Perkins. Maybe some blood dripping out of the card slot? Some slime oozing down the side?"

"No. It's just..." He glances at the big glass doors. It's dark inside, since the bank's been closed for half an hour now, except for some low-level lighting that I guess is meant to scare away burglars. "It looks like an office building."

"It *is* an office building."

He stares up at it. It's so tall, he has to lean his head back to take it all in. "Wow." Then he looks at me, his eyebrows coming together in concern, though he doesn't actually say anything.

He doesn't have to. I know what he's thinking. I filled him in in the car on the way here, about what happened with Pete. Well, the gist of it, anyway, which included the part about me falling from the top of this place. "It wasn't so bad," I lie, because I can't stand him looking at me like that. Like he feels sorry for me.

"It's an awfully long way to fall."

"No one said it wasn't."

"I just mean, I'd be really freaked out. If I fell from there."

"If you fell from there, you'd be dead." Just like Pete.

"I can see how you'd be traumatized. How *anyone* would, even if they weren't afraid of heights. That's all."

I wish he didn't know about that. I thought I was okay with it—with him knowing—but now I'm not so sure. "So, according to you, I'm just messed up. Is that it?"

He looks almost hurt by that. "Come on, X. You know that's not what I'm saying."

"Do I? Because it sounds like that's *exactly* what you're saying."

He sighs. "From what you've told me, some really bad things happened to you here. Probably some of the worst moments of your life. So it's understandable if you... you know."

"If I'm messed up. Yeah, I got that."

"If it's hard for you to be here."

"Well, that's where you're wrong, because it's not." I shrug, just to show how much I don't care, even if it's a lie.

"You almost died here. Kat and Sarah almost died here. And your friend actually *did* die here."

"I told you, he wasn't my friend. He tried to *kill* me. I was under mind control, and he ordered me to jump off the ledge! And that was before he knew I could fly. He had no idea I was going to survive that, but he made me do it anyway, and he didn't even flinch."

"You're upset about it." It's not a question.

I want to tell him it's none of his business, and it's *not*, but I stop myself, because it seems mean to say that when he came all the way down here with me. "Yep. I'm upset about it, and there are no signs of any ghosts here, so I think we can all draw our conclusions about that." Maybe the reason Kat didn't hear Pete's voice wasn't because she was too far away, but because she's not as messed up about what happened as I am. Maybe she's moved on, or it wasn't as traumatic for her, or her mom didn't also betray her and disown her on the same night. Who knows.

Riley glances over at the ATM, looking kind of disappointed. Maybe a ghost would have been more exciting than the more realistic answer—that I'm completely losing it. "Do you want to talk about it?"

"We talked about it on the way here."

"You told me an outline of what happened. You didn't tell me *why* it happened, or, like, how you felt?"

A drop of rain lands on my nose. It's just one drop at first, but then another hits my hand. "We should go."

"Okay, but it might help to—"

"It won't. So just drop it." He wants to know how I felt about it? Awful, that's how. Which should be obvious enough already. And as for why it happened... Pete was a jerk. And he was probably never really my friend. Nothing that Riley can't guess. He doesn't need to hear how Kat cheated on me with my supposed best friend and how much that hurt.

The rain's coming down harder, but Riley doesn't move to leave. "You can trust me. You know that, right? We're friends."

"Yeah, well, I trusted Pete, too, and look how that turned out. Being friends obviously doesn't mean that much." I didn't know I was going to say that. As soon as the words leave my mouth, I wish I could take them back. Riley's nothing like Pete. More like his exact opposite.

Shock spreads across Riley's face, just for a second, and then changes to sadness. He moves to leave.

"Perkins, wait. I didn't mean—"

"You're right—we should go. It's raining."

"But—"

"You made it pretty clear that you don't have anything to say to me. So just don't, okay?"

"We hardly even looked for the ghost. We came all the way down here."

"You're the one who said we should leave. And that there weren't any signs of any ghosts."

I swallow. He hasn't said he's pissed at me, or that I screwed up, but I still feel like the worst friend in the world. "But—"

"Let's just go home."

I suck in a deep breath, taking that in. "Yeah, okay. If that's what you—"

But before I can finish that sentence, all the lights in the Banking and Finances building suddenly shut off. So does the ATM. Except, unlike the lights inside, it immediately flashes back on.

Giant letters fill the screen that say, *HAPPY BIRTHDAY*.

Sparks of electricity run up my spine. Pete said that to me here, on the last night he was alive, referencing the fact that our friendship ended on my fifteenth birthday, when I caught him making out with Kat. Seeing it now is *not* reassuring.

Then Pete's voice comes out of the ATM speaker. It's a little tinny, but mostly clear, and I know Riley hears it, too, judging by the freaked out look on his face. "Damien," Pete says, "it's about time. Welcome back, birthday boy. We've got so much to catch up on."

As soon as he says that, there's a loud *click*, and then one of the big glass doors falls open, inviting us into the darkness.

X·X·X

I've seen enough horror movies to know that nothing good can come from going inside this building, but I do it anyway. Because, seriously, what am I going to do, *walk away*? I'd spend the rest of my life wondering what the hell was going on. It's one thing to have heard Pete's voice yesterday, or at least to think I did. After a while, I could probably have convinced myself that it didn't actually happen. But this is different.

This is a lot harder to ignore, especially since Riley obviously heard and saw everything, too.

"I thought you were leaving," I whisper, once we're inside. Whispering seems like the right thing to do, even though Pete's ghost can probably still hear me. Not that he's actually a ghost, because that's impossible. Or at least I thought it was, up until a minute ago. I'm starting to have my doubts.

"Are you serious?" Riley whispers back.

"You didn't have to come with me."

"There's no way I was letting you go in here alone. I came to check this out with you, and that's what I'm doing. Even if you don't want me here."

"I didn't say that."

"Okay. Good." He sounds relieved.

And as much as this isn't Riley's problem, and as much as he should probably be making a run for it while he still can, I'm kind of glad he's here. Because I don't actually want to be alone with a ghost. At the Golden City Banking and Finances building. On Halloween.

"Okay, Pete," I say, mostly to the ceiling, since I don't know how to address someone I can't see. And now that I'm not whispering, my voice sounds way too loud in the empty room. "I'm here. So—"

Me and Riley both jump as the door slams shut behind us. There's another *click* as it locks.

Whose idea was it to come in here again?

I make electricity flicker along my hand, just so we're not totally in the dark. And in case any ghosts come flying at me, because there's a chance they can still get fried, just like anybody else, and I want to be prepared.

"*That's* new," Pete says. His voice comes out of all the computers on everyone's desks, each one at a different volume, so that it sounds like there are a dozen of him talking at once. "Last time I checked, you only had that

filthy hero power. I guess you really are a mixed breed."
He laughs.

"Are you *sure* he died?" Riley whispers.

"*Yes*. I'm sure." This whole scenario would be a lot less creepy if it turned out Pete was still alive and was just messing with me—and he'd be for sure zappable—but he hit the pavement from, like, a million stories up. I made a point not to look at the body, but there definitely was one. And a funeral, which I wasn't invited to, for obvious reasons.

"Oh, I'm dead all right," Pete says. "My boy here killed me."

Lightning surges in my hand, no longer just sparks. "That's not what happened."

"'Course, he couldn't do it himself. Had to get his little sidekick and his mommy to do it for him."

"Your sidekick?" Riley asks, and there's just enough light that I can see the worry on his face.

"Sarah didn't kill anyone."

"Tried to, though, didn't she?" Pete says. "She was so desperate to save you."

"To save all of us," I correct him.

He ignores me. "And here it is, hasn't even been a year, and you've already replaced me. Perkins, is it?"

Anger flares in my chest when he calls Riley that. "Shut up, Pete. You don't get to talk to him."

"*Oh.* See, now that's why you're here in the first place. You think you can control everybody, tell them what to do."

"What's he talking about?" Riley whispers.

28

Pete laughs again, his voice echoing across the computers. "Great question! I'm so glad you asked. Are you keeping score here, Damien? That's one point for the new friend—not that you ever really *have* friends—and zero for you."

"What the hell do you want, Pete?!"

"I want to play a little game. Perkins can play, too."

Lightning crackles along my skin. "We're not playing any games."

"Oh, yes, you are. You see, you're not calling the shots anymore. The whole time I knew you, we always had to do what *you* wanted. Not tonight. Tonight, you do what I say, or you don't get out of here."

I look behind me at the glass doors. They might be locked, but that wouldn't stop a blast of lightning. "I can leave whenever I want. You're not keeping us here."

"Here are the rules. I'm going to ask you a few questions, and all you have to do is tell the truth."

"That's all?" Riley asks, sounding pretty skeptical.

"Look at that," Pete says, and I can hear the smile in his voice. "Seems like you don't know him so well, after all. This is going to be fun. Way better than that Halloween when Damien convinced me to give him all my candy. You remember that?"

"That was a long time ago. We were still trick-or-treating. And you could have said no."

"So it's my fault you're a manipulative bastard? It's *my* fault you never think about anybody but yourself, huh? Shouldn't surprise me, coming from you."

"It wasn't all of your candy, either. Only some of it."

"Only the ones *you* liked. You said there was an outbreak of food poisoning and that those brands were being recalled. You said your mom had a way to test for it."

"You said that?" Riley asks, sounding way too shocked for someone who's known me for more than five minutes.

"*He's* the one who believed it."

"We were eleven!" Pete shouts. All the computers turn up to full volume.

"We don't have to do this," I tell Riley. Then, to Pete, "I'm not playing your stupid game. We're getting out of here."

"Think again, Damien. I've got security footage of you breaking in."

"We didn't break in."

The computer monitors flicker on. A black and white video of me and Riley plays on the screens. We're at the door, looking kind of nervous and glancing over our shoulders before going inside.

Then the image on the screens changes. All the computers start scrolling through spreadsheets like crazy.

"I suppose you didn't access all these financial records, either."

Crap. "That's all you've got to keep me here? Blackmail?"

"*You* can call it that. The police will call it *evidence*."

Riley glances at me, then at the door. "Come on, X. Let's just go. We'll figure out how to explain this later."

"X," Pete says. "That's cute. But it's going to be hard to explain why *X* here blasted through those doors. Anyone could come in and take all these files. But maybe that's what you had planned all along."

"Come on," Riley says again. "He's just making guesses. We don't know what will happen."

No, we don't. But Pete's guesses of us getting in trouble make a lot more sense than Riley's blind faith that we can somehow explain this away. Because, honestly? The explanation for why we're really here doesn't paint me in a very good light. It kind of sounds like a recipe for ending up in an asylum, or at least in extensive court-mandated therapy, which I'd really like to avoid.

"I'll stay," I tell Pete, "but Riley goes free."

Riley shakes his head. "I'm not going anywhere."

"You hear that?" Pete says. "He's not going anywhere. That's two points for Perkins so far."

"Let him go. I mean it, Pete."

"You mean it. Ha. Stop pretending that you care about anyone besides yourself. Perkins stays, X. As my replacement, I think he's going to want to hear what I have to say."

CHAPTER 4

"You remember that summer when I was fifteen and you were fourteen?" Pete asks.

It's a simple enough question, but I already don't like where this is going. "Yeah, I remember. We went swimming almost every day. And that ice cream place got that new flavor, raspberry hazelnut crunch, and we ate so much of it, we couldn't even say the word *raspberry* without gagging."

It ended up being a running joke between us at the end of the summer. Whenever things got too quiet or we wanted to change the subject, one of us would say *raspberry* or *hazelnut* and we'd bust up laughing.

"Those were good times," Pete agrees, and from the tone of his voice, I think he actually means it.

Riley studies my face, probably wondering what the hell we're talking about or what this has to do with me being a selfish bastard.

"The truth is," I say to Pete, "that really was a great

summer. Maybe even my best summer. And it was definitely—"

"Don't." There's no nostalgia in his voice now. No trace that anything from that summer was a happy memory for him, even though I know it must have been. "What did I tell you about lying?"

I lean against the edge of one of the desks, careful not to get my fingerprints on anything, because I'm already going to have enough trouble explaining this if we get caught. "You said you were going to ask me some questions. Well, you asked me one, and I gave you an honest answer."

He laughs. Not, like, a happy laugh or anything. It's more like the kind of laugh a murderer would have right before he chopped you up. "That was *a* question. It wasn't *the* question. But you knew that, Damien. Always trying to weasel your way out of everything—that's you. And don't tell me it was your best summer ever."

It was, though. At least, it was the best summer we spent together. It was also the last, and maybe the fact that it's something I can never get back makes it seem better than it was. "Ask me *the* question, then. And hurry it up. We have places to be."

"X," Riley warns, like he doesn't think it's a good idea to provoke a ghost who already has a grudge against me. He's probably right.

"Watching out for him, huh?" Pete says. "I don't know you, Perkins, but trust me—I'm doing you a huge favor tonight."

I shove my hands in my pockets and clench my fists.

"Ask the question, Pete."

"Yeah? You ready for this? If you remember that summer, then you remember I was supposed to spend it with my grandma. She lived out in the country, near my aunt and uncle and all my cousins, and I was going to go stay with her. But that didn't happen."

"Plans change. That's life. You probably had more fun with me, anyway."

"Shut up!" All the lights flash on and off a couple times, totally exposing us to anyone walking by.

Me and Riley duck down behind the desks. I peer at the doors, checking if there's anyone out there who might have seen us. "What the hell are you doing, Pete?!"

"Don't act like you don't know, like you're not the *reason* I didn't go to my grandma's that summer."

So he knows about that. I want to ask him how he found out, but that seems counterproductive. "I did you a favor! You would have been bored, stuck out in the country for three months. You would have hated it."

"No, I wouldn't. And my grandma died that winter. Do you remember *that*?"

Riley sucks in his breath.

"It turned out that was my last chance to see her," Pete goes on. "I could have spent a whole summer with her, and instead, I never even got to see her again before she died."

"I..." I felt horrible about that, not that Pete would believe me if I told him.

"He couldn't have known," Riley says.

Pete scoffs. "And how do you know that? You weren't

there."

Riley looks me in the eyes. "Because if he'd known, he wouldn't have done whatever he did to keep you from going."

"It's true." It's not like Pete's grandma was particularly old or sickly or anything. She *seemed* fine. I didn't know she was going to get pneumonia, and I certainly didn't know she was going to die from it.

Pete acts like he didn't hear me. "I found out months later that he talked to my parents behind my back and convinced them there was this girl I liked. That she and I were, like, made for each other, and I'd be heartbroken if I went away for the summer and lost her, and that I was just too polite or embarrassed to tell them. You *know* how messed up that is, Damien, because when there really was a girl I liked, you didn't help me get her. You went and stabbed me right in the back. But there's plenty of time for that later. Right now, we're talking about how you stole my last chance to spend time with my grandma."

"Nobody knows when anybody else is going to die," Riley says, still defending me.

"I didn't know you were never going to get to see her again, Pete. There's no way I could have. And if I had—"

"I don't care about your excuses! You didn't know, but it doesn't matter, because you were *always* taking things from me! So I just want to know why. What the hell was so important that you manipulated my parents into keeping me home for the summer?"

"I..."

"Come on, Damien!" Pete makes the lights flash again,

only this time they don't stop.

"I didn't want to spend the summer alone, okay?! You were my best friend!"

"Not good enough!"

"It's the truth!"

"There's more than that. Better tell me, or someone's going to notice all these lights and come find you. Oh, there's someone now, wondering what the hell's going on. She hasn't reached for her phone yet, but it's only a matter of time."

"What Damien did was wrong," Riley says to Pete, "but it's understandable. The not wanting to be alone part."

"I think I know my boy better than that. Oh, and, Damien? She's pulling out her phone, and I don't think she's texting a friend. The truth. *Now.*"

Damn it. "You want to know the real reason? When my mom heard you weren't going to be around for the summer, she decided that meant I was going to paint the house and pull weeds and help her rearrange her lab. I would have been stuck doing manual labor for three months. That's why I made sure you'd be in town. It was selfish, and manipulative, but I did it anyway. Is that what you want to hear?!"

Pete's quiet, like he's thinking that over. The lights go dim and stop flashing.

Riley's looking at me like... Like he's surprised I'd do something that awful to someone I supposedly cared about.

Still, it seems like Pete bought it. And even if Riley thinks I'm a terrible person, well, at least he doesn't actually know *how* terrible.

But just when I think Pete's satisfied with my answer, the lights start flashing again. "You expect me to believe that?! Your mom's never painted her house. And you would have found a way out of it if she did. I don't think you understand the rules of this game, Damien. Three seconds, and I pull the fire alarm, and then it doesn't matter if the woman outside calls the cops or not!"

He's bluffing. Even though he's a ghost and has absolutely nothing to lose and everything to gain by getting me in trouble.

"One."

"It's the truth! I could have gotten out of that stuff some other way, but then I still would have been alone."

"Two."

Crap.

"Come on, X," Riley whispers, pleading with me. "Whatever it is, it's okay."

It's not, though.

"Thr—"

"It was because of your cousins!" The words just burst out of me, and I don't know if saying them makes me feel better or worse. "Every time you stayed at your grandma's house, all you could talk about for weeks afterward was how great your cousins and their friends were. You made it clear that when you were there, with them, you didn't need me. You liked them *better* than me. And if you'd spent three whole months with them... You never would have shut up about it. You probably would have ditched me for good. And that's why I did it. Why I made sure you'd be home for the summer. With me."

The lights stop. Before it goes dark, I catch sight of Riley's expression and the way his mouth hangs open in shock.

"See?" Pete says. "All you had to do was admit what a horrible bastard you are. And hey, if it makes you feel any better, it's not like I didn't already know. I mean, it looks like Perkins didn't, but he would have figured it out eventually, after you screwed him over a few times."

It's dark now, and my eyes haven't adjusted, so I can't see if Riley still looks horrified. I could use my lightning to check, but it might attract attention from outside, and the truth is, I kind of don't want to know.

"That was Round One," Pete says, right as the elevator dings and the doors slide open. "Are you ready for Round Two?"

CHAPTER 5

We get in the elevator. It's probably the stupidest thing we've done all night. But it doesn't go anywhere, and at least we can have the lights on in here without anyone calling the police. Still, this is Pete we're dealing with, and I know better than to let my guard down.

"You know what I want to talk about now?" Pete asks. There's just the one speaker for his voice to come out of, so it no longer sounds like there's a dozen of him. "I want to talk about Kat. And how you stole her from me."

I open my mouth to argue with that, but Riley beats me to it. "That's such crap," he says, shaking his head. "You can't *steal* someone."

Pete laughs. "So I take it you and him have never liked the same girl? If you had, you wouldn't still be friends."

"I wouldn't say that."

"*Perkins*." I tilt my head, trying to signal for him to shut up.

"Oh, no," Pete says. "I want to hear this."

Riley shrugs. "He and Sarah went out for, like, a week."

"Sarah. As in, his *sidekick*?"

"It was back before I even knew her. Or Damien. I mean, I didn't know either of them. That's how we met, because of Sarah, and... Let me start over. They were friends, it didn't even take a week for Sarah to realize they should stay that way, and she broke up with him. Nothing even happened. Right, X?"

He tries to meet my eyes. I glance away without thinking. My heart speeds up, and this elevator suddenly feels way too small for two people. There's a tense silence that makes me wish I was anywhere but here right now.

An edge of fear creeps into Riley's voice. "Are you saying something *did* happen?"

"I'm not saying anything. It doesn't even matter now."

Pete's clearly enjoying this. "Sounds like it matters to Perkins here. Sounds like it matters a lot."

"Tell me," Riley says.

"You don't really want to know. It's just going to bother you."

"X. *Tell me.*"

I swallow. I make myself not look away this time. "We made out."

He takes that in. It's obviously not good news, but not the end of the world, either. "Is that all?"

"A lot. We made out a lot. That was kind of the whole point of our relationship, because... Listen, Perkins, you don't need to hear this. It was stupid."

"Did you sleep with her?" His voice gets too high when

he asks that.

"No. *No.* She wanted to. Eventually. She had this plan…"

Riley's face is red. He leans against the elevator wall, his fists clenched at his sides. "She wanted to sleep with you. With *you.* After a *week.*"

"See," Pete says, "now we're getting somewhere. Go on, Damien. Tell him what you did with his girl."

"Nothing!"

Riley presses his palms to his forehead. "We've been going out for five months, and we haven't… We've talked about it. I think, maybe soon, but… God, X. *A week?!* No, not a week. Because that's when you *broke up.*"

"We were just messing around! That was the whole point. Sarah wanted to experiment."

"Experiment." Now he looks like he's going to be sick.

"It wasn't a big deal."

"Not a big deal?! Did you kiss her? Did you have your tongue in her mouth? Were your hands on her?!"

I don't answer, which is answer enough.

"Don't tell me it wasn't a big deal. I thought you and Sarah just hung out. That you maybe went out to dinner or something."

"Now *that* we didn't do."

He glares at me. "And now I find out that you were going to sleep with her. That that was the whole reason you were even together. Not because you were friends, but because she wanted to have sex with you?"

When he puts it that way… "Perkins, come on."

"Have you and her…" He swallows. "You said you

didn't have sex, but did you… Did you get close to it?"

"No! Look, it wasn't a one-week plan. It was a *two-month* plan. And I don't think Sarah was really that serious about it, anyway. She liked me, and she didn't know how to tell me."

"So she thought she'd just sleep with you?!"

"It didn't mean anything! It wasn't anything like what you guys have. And if she hasn't slept with you, it's because you're actually important to her, so—"

"I know that! I don't need *you* to tell me that!" He lets his head fall back against the wall and scrubs at his face with his hands. "Why did it end?"

I look down at my shoes. The carpet in the elevator is gray with black swirls in it. I wrap my arms around myself. "I was in love with Kat."

"But you were going to sleep with Sarah." Riley's voice is heavy with disappointment. And disgust.

Guilt squirms in my chest, and my face feels too hot. I wish I wasn't in this elevator, so I could go find a hole to crawl into.

A slow clap plays through the speaker. "Aaaaaand, scene. That was great, Damien. You dug yourself in real good—you didn't even need my help. What did I tell you, Perkins? Not so eager to defend him now, are you? And that only took, oh, about five minutes."

"Perkins." My voice comes out strained, and I hate that Pete's hearing any of this. "It wasn't what you think."

Riley stares into the corner, avoiding me. "You and Sarah didn't break up because there was nothing between you. You broke up because *you* were in love with someone else."

"I didn't know I was in love with Kat. I should have, but I didn't, because... Because I didn't want to know. Things were complicated between us—"

"*Complicated*," Pete says. "Is that what you call it when your girl cheats on you with your best friend?"

Riley looks up at that.

I clench my jaw, trying to ignore Pete. "I wasn't trying to sleep with Sarah, okay?"

"But you would have done it anyway," Riley says.

"Or," Pete continues, "is *complicated* when you best friend goes out with the girl he *knows* you like and doesn't care?"

"I don't know what I would have done," I tell Riley. "Maybe I would have gone through with it, but..." I run a hand through my hair and let out a deep breath. "It wouldn't have felt right, with Sarah. And for what it's worth, I'm glad that we didn't get that far. I'm glad that I lost it with Kat."

"Wait." Riley glances over at me. "You were a virgin?"

I really wish Pete wasn't listening to this. Not that it's news to him, but still. "Yeah. I was."

"But you... You're always..."

"He's always messing around where he shouldn't be." Pete sounds pissed again, and the elevator suddenly jerks upward. "Always trying to make people think he's something he's not."

My stomach lurches toward the floor, and I grab hold of the metal bar that's against the wall. I remember this being the slowest elevator ever, but now it's going up *really* fast. Because Pete has control of it.

What's Kat going to think when she reads my obituary and finds out I came back to the Banking and Finances building and *died*? I mean, hopefully someone would tell her before she saw it in the paper—especially since Kat doesn't even read the paper—but either way, she's going to be pissed. And heartbroken. And probably really confused about what I was even doing here.

"Don't be fooled, man," Pete says. "Virgin or not, he would have done it with her and moved on, and he wouldn't have lost any sleep over it."

"That's not..." That's not what would have happened. I know it's not. "Just ask your stupid question."

"My stupid question?! You don't get it, do you? You're going to play my game"—the elevator stops moving up and then *drops* down a ways instead, far enough that I feel like the floor's falling out from under me, and like I'm going to die—"or you're going to suffer the consequences."

Elevators don't usually bother me the way stairs do, but this is different. My heart races, and lightning crackles along my skin.

Riley shoots me a worried look, though I can't tell if he's worried about me, or about me blowing up the place. He takes a step away from the metal bar that runs along the wall, probably so I won't accidentally electrocute him.

"Flying's not going to save you in here." There's a smugness in Pete's voice that makes me wish he was still alive, so I could punch him in the face. "You knew I liked Kat. The only reason you even met her was because I introduced you to her. Because I *liked* her. I told you that. I told you how I felt about her, and *you*—"

The elevator drops again, farther this time.

I slump down to the floor and wrap my arms around my knees. I hate this. I hate this so much. And I really, *really* hate Pete.

"Oops," he says. "Guess I got carried away. Didn't mean to freak you out. Oh, wait, *yes, I did.*"

"You didn't need to do that." Riley glares at the speaker where Pete's voice is coming from, then at the security camera above us. "He's answering your questions, and you didn't need to do that!"

Pete's voice has a nasty tone to it, and the elevator shakes a little with each word. "Stay. Out. Of. It."

"It's going to be okay," Riley says to me.

"What the hell is wrong with you?!" Pete shouts, and I hate to agree with him, but I was kind of thinking the same thing. "He was going to sleep with your girl! He was going to use her, just like he uses everybody!"

Riley scowls at that—at *me*—but he doesn't say anything.

Him defending me at all at this point is probably more than I deserve. Even if he only did it because I'm huddled in a ball on the floor and he must have felt sorry for me. "You want answers, Pete? Stop shaking the damned elevator and ask me your question already."

"Why'd you go after Kat, huh?"

"Kat made her own choices."

"No. I didn't ask why she ended up with you, I asked why *you* went after her. You knew I liked her. But you didn't say, 'Hey, Pete, is she, like, the love of your life or something? Because maybe I like her, too. Let's talk about this.' Nope. The second you met her, you flirted with her like crazy. You started hanging out with her behind my back. As if me liking her meant absolutely nothing to you! Like *I* meant nothing to you. You were supposed to be my best friend, but you didn't care about me. We'd been friends since we were kids, but you were willing to throw all that away the second you met her."

The elevator drops a little farther. I shut my eyes and press my forehead into my knees. Sparks of lightning prickle along my back.

"You screwed me over every chance you got. Hell, you probably took Kat just to show me you could. To prove that you always win, and I always end up with nothing. Was that it?!"

I cringe, waiting for the elevator to drop again, but it doesn't this time. Instead, it starts moving up higher. "I wasn't— I didn't mean to flirt with her."

"So you admit that you were."

"It just happened. And she flirted back. And then... It wouldn't have worked out between you two, anyway."

"You think you get to decide that? That because you tell yourself that, it makes it okay?!"

"Kat liked *me*. She wasn't into you!"

"You never gave her a chance to be into me!"

"We just clicked, okay? And we started hanging out, and before I knew it, we were together. I didn't even know if you still liked her by then."

"Because I hardly ever saw you. Because you always

chose her over me."

The elevator stops. The number for the top floor lights up, though the doors stay closed.

Riley exchanges a look with me. I can't tell if he's trying to ask if I have a plan, or if he's just confirming that we're screwed.

Which I'm pretty sure we are.

"But then," Pete says, "there was that time *she* chose me over you. At your own birthday party. When you were still going out with her."

Rage boils up inside me. I hate him for doing this, and I hate him for bringing that up. "She was upset. It was a mistake."

"That's funny, because she told me that going out with *you* was the mistake. You know, maybe if you'd cared that I liked her before you took her from me, I might have cared that she was still with you when I made out with her."

"That's so messed up. You want to talk about caring about somebody? You never cared about Kat. Ever."

The elevator shakes. "Say that again, Damien. I dare you."

Riley's eyes widen. "Dude," he whispers, but I pretend like I don't hear.

"If you cared about her, you wouldn't have taken her hostage! You wouldn't have made out with her when you knew she was with me! And you wouldn't have let your friends grope her at your party!"

"Let them? What happened to 'Kat made her own choices'? And the way I remember it, she was the one begging them."

"She was drunk! And she was hurting." Because I told her there was nothing between us, that there never could be, even though I knew it was a lie.

"Yeah, and she's the one who drank all my booze like I'm made of money, even though nobody even invited her. She's the one who acted like a skank, too. All on her own."

"She came to you vulnerable, and what did you do?" Lightning zaps across my arms and surges in my hands. It makes my hair stand on end. I get to my feet, because I'm not going to say this from the floor. "You know what those guys were going to do to her. She couldn't say no, and you weren't going to stop them. If I hadn't shown up—" My voice shakes. So do my hands. "You want to claim that I don't care about anybody? You *never* cared about Kat! You can be pissed all you want that I ended up with her, but the truth is, you were never good enough for her!"

Pete's voice is harsh and cold. "Wrong answer, Damien."

And then the elevator drops into a free fall.

CHAPTER 6

I take back what I said earlier. Getting in this elevator
was *definitely* the stupidest thing we've done all night.
Possibly in our entire lives, which are about to end.

I feel like I don't weigh anything. This is so much worse
than falling off the top of the building. At least then I
could see how much farther I had before I hit the ground.
And of course I could fly. Just barely, but it was enough to
save myself. It won't help here, like Pete said, plus, even if
it would, it wouldn't help Riley.

He's going to die because of me.

He's going to die thinking I'm a bad person, and hating
me for how I treated Sarah. And maybe I deserve that.
Maybe Pete's right about me, and I did ruin things
between us. But I'm not going to let that happen with
Riley.

"Perkins, I—"

A horrible screeching sound of metal on metal
interrupts me and fills my ears as the elevator's brakes

kick in, trying to slow us down. It's the worst sound I've ever heard. The whole elevator shakes, like it's going to fall apart. I don't feel weightless anymore, and the change in speed slams both me and Riley to the floor. I lie down, bracing myself for impact, and hold my breath until my lungs ache. Riley does the same.

It's not slowing fast enough. We're going to hit the ground. We're going to *hit the ground*.

And then—

We don't. The elevator stops moving. The brakes stop screeching.

"Just kidding," Pete says, and there's this manic edge in his voice that makes me think it took effort for him not to kill us. "You didn't think you'd get off that easy, did you?"

I pick myself up off the floor. I'm covered in sweat, and all my muscles are trembling. My heart's beating way too fast. But I'm alive. And so is Riley.

"Nah," Pete goes on. "After everything you've done to me, where's the fun in that?"

The elevator starts moving up again.

He's going to drop us over and over, until the brakes stop working or he makes a mistake. Or until he decides he's had enough. And then we're both dead. But that's assuming I don't freak out, go all electric, and accidentally obliterate Riley first.

And all that because luring me here and trying to kill my friends wasn't good enough the first time. He had to come back from the *dead* and try to do it again. Anger and hatred burn in my chest. Lightning washes over my skin.

"You can throw me down as many times as you want,

Pete, but it won't change the facts!"

"*Us*," Riley says. "You're going to get us *both* killed."

"Kat liked me better! She never even saw you that way!"

The elevator shakes. Pete's voice is a low growl. "Watch your mouth."

"It's been years, and you still can't stop whining about it? That's just sad."

Riley glares at me. "Will you shut the hell up?!"

"This isn't about Kat," Pete says. "This is about *you*. And I'd listen to your... Well, maybe *friend* isn't the right word. Not after tonight."

"Fine. You're not mad that Kat picked me, you're mad that I ditched you. That I moved on. With a personality like yours, Pete, I'm surprised it didn't happen sooner!"

"X." Riley's eyes meet mine, dead serious about this. "Stop. Talking."

I ignore him, still addressing Pete. "In fact, you're lucky I hung around with you as long as I did!"

Pete screams in rage. The elevator drops a little ways.

"*Dude!*" Riley's so mad, he's shaking, and I think he might try and tackle me if I wasn't covered in lightning. "Shut up already!"

I don't think I've ever seen Riley this pissed at me. I stare at him, not because I'm shutting up like he wants, but because I'm not sure what to say.

"Knew that was coming," Pete says. "But you've got to ask yourself something, Damien. Is Perkins this mad because you won't keep your mouth shut, or because you can't keep your hands to yourself?"

Riley glances away.

The elevator starts moving up again. "Can't say I blame him. Finding out that his girl wanted you first, that she had *plans* for you? That's rough, man. He's probably wondering if she ever regrets not getting her chance with you. If she wishes she'd seen you naked so she doesn't have to use her imagina—"

"That's enough, Pete!" I shout. "Sarah's not... She doesn't think about me like that." Not anymore.

"And what about you? You were into her little plan— you must have had the same thoughts about her."

Riley cringes. His face is red, and he can't even look at me.

Pete keeps going. "Doesn't matter if Perkins has gotten farther with her. He's always going to know that before she did anything with him, she pictured every detail about what it would be like to do it with *you*."

"You don't know that!" I clench my fists to keep myself from zapping the speaker, because all I want right now is for him to shut up. But Pete getting the chance to torture us is probably the only reason he hasn't killed us yet.

"She'll be comparing what it's like with him with how she thought it would be with you. Be honest, Damien— some part of you is just *loving* that."

"No."

Riley looks over at me, watching my face, like there's even any chance that Pete's right.

The elevator reaches the top floor. The doors stay closed, and this is it—Pete's going to drop us again, only I don't know if he'll catch us this time, or if the brakes are even still intact enough to save us if he did.

Pete makes a buzzer sound, like when someone gets something wrong on a game show. "Try again. You know the rules—give me the truth this time."

"You think I'm enjoying this?!"

"The truth, Damien, or you both die!"

I glance over at Riley.

He looks so miserable. He practically spits the words, "Just tell him." And I hate the way he says it, like he thinks I'm lying.

"I don't care what you want to hear, Pete! I've already told you the truth! And you can kill me if you want, but let Riley go."

"But just look at his face," Pete says. "It looks kind of like yours did when you walked in on me and Kat. And I sure as hell enjoyed that—that was pure gold. I wish I'd had a camera."

I wince at the memory. "That's you, not me."

"If that's your final answer..."

I shut my eyes. I brace myself, even though I know it's pointless. Thoughts race through my head, of all the things I should tell Riley before we die. But there are too many, and I don't know what to say, only that if we're going to die, I don't want it to be with him hating me.

But then there's a *ding*, and the elevator doors slide open.

"Congratulations!" Pete says, in a fake announcer voice. "You've made it to our last and final round! And, Damien, I *do* mean final. Everybody ready? There's no going back now. You've got about five seconds before I drop this elevator. If you want to keep playing, I suggest you get the hell out."

X·X·X

We dive through the open doors, into a hallway on the top floor, right before the elevator falls.

That could have been us. I glance over at Riley, trying to convey how glad I am that we're not dead—something I'm pretty sure he can relate to—but he's too busy taking in our surroundings to notice. Or just pretending to, because he's ignoring me, since he hates my guts now.

"Welcome to Round Three!" Pete says. "Some of our contestants might remember a little incident that took place here a few months ago. And by *some*, I mean you, Damien."

Something twitches on the ceiling. I look up and see a weapon aiming at us.

"Um. Perkins."

Riley pretends like he doesn't hear me.

I elbow him.

"*What, X?!* What do you—" He sees what I'm looking at and shuts up.

"After that 'little incident,'" Pete goes on, "the building owners decided to up security. Someone *died* here, after all. They couldn't look like they didn't care and do nothing. So they had these little babies installed."

There are some whirring sounds as a couple more weapons spaced out across the ceiling move to point at us.

"They're just supposed to burn a little, but that's not

how this game is played. So I cranked them up. *Way* up. Now, I'm not saying that a blast from one of these will kill you"—he laughs a little as the weapons charge up—"but I wouldn't want to get hit with one. If I was, you know, *still alive.*"

Crap.

A green laser suddenly shoots at us.

I duck just in time. Riley turns invisible. He doesn't cry out or anything, so I assume he also got out of the way.

"Invisibility, huh?" Pete says. A couple of the lasers aim toward what looks like empty space. "Good thing these security cameras can see IR."

"Perkins, watch out!"

The lasers fire. Riley turns visible again as he scrambles out of the way.

"What the hell, Pete?!" I shout at the ceiling. "What are you—"

I jump to one side as another laser fires at me. I look over at Riley, and this time he actually makes eye contact. Neither of us has to say anything. We just start running.

Pete's voice follows us down the hall and into the main room of the office, playing across intercoms and out of computers on people's desks. "See, now, I'm such a good friend that I remembered how much you hate stairs. Think you can get down all seventy-six flights? Think you can get down even *one*?"

A laser barely misses us, singeing the wall next to me instead. And no, there's no way in hell I could get down that many flights of stairs, even on a good day. One where I hadn't just been dropped in an elevator, and where I didn't also have lasers flying at me. I mean, maybe there aren't lasers in the stairwell, but I kind of doubt it. Pete sounds way too happy about all this for that to be true, like he's got me right where he wants me.

"Oh, and, Damien? The police are here. They're only on the first floor, but even if you make it that far in one piece —which, let's face it, you *won't*—they'll be waiting to arrest you." He laughs like that's the funniest thing ever.

Riley shoves me out of the way as another laser almost hits us. We duck behind a wall that separates the main part of the office from the bathrooms, resting for a second as we try to catch our breath. My arm kind of hurts where Riley shoved me, and even though he saved me from getting burned by a laser, I think maybe he didn't have to push so hard.

He looks me over, like he's summing me up and I'm coming up short. "That's a lot of stairs," he says.

What he means is, there's no way I can make it. Not like I needed him to tell me that. I shake my head. "We're not... Pete wants us going down them."

"So he can shoot at us the whole way. And if we don't get *killed*, we get arrested." Riley scowls at me, as if he can't believe I got him into this.

Technically, he's the one who said we should come down here, but I don't bring that up.

Pete's voice echoes out across all the computers. "When are you going to get it? You can't hide from me."

Lasers blast against the wall right next to our heads.

We keep running.

"We can't do what he wants," I tell Riley. "We're not

going down those stairs."

"And you want to do what? Stay here?!"

A laser grazes the edge of his coat, leaving a singe mark.

"The roof," I whisper, in between breaths. Just the thought of it leaves a bad taste in my mouth. "We're going to the roof."

"We're *what*?!"

"Believe me, it's the last place I want to go. But it's—"

"No whispering!" Pete shouts. A laser hits the heel of my shoe and sends me sprawling. It doesn't hurt—the laser doesn't, anyway; my chin hitting the floor is another story—but it leaves my foot way too warm.

I roll out of the way of another blast that's aimed at my face. It all happens really quickly, and then Riley's grabbing my arm and pulling me to my feet.

My heart's racing. I could be wrong about this, and if my plan doesn't work... "Think about it," I tell Riley, trying to keep my voice down. "He talks to us through speakers. He sees us with the security cameras."

Understanding washes across Riley's face. "There won't be any of those on the roof."

And no lasers. At least, I hope not. "Either we get a break, or—"

"He'll have to show himself."

I mime blasting someone with my hands. Not that I'm crazy about actually *seeing* Pete, or about having to face him head on without knowing if I can really zap him or not, but at least then we'd have a chance. Running for our lives is getting old, and it's only a matter of time before one of us gets blasted for reals. And I didn't survive that night here seven months ago just so Pete's freaking ghost could come back and finish the job.

"What's that?" Pete says. He must have noticed my hand gesture. "What did you just say to him?!"

We turn a corner into the hallway with the roof access door. I don't know if Pete's figured out what our goal is, or if he's just still trying to kill us in general, but four lasers fire in a row at the ground ahead of us, forcing us back.

"It's not going to work," Riley says. "He *knows*."

If that's true, it means Pete doesn't want us going up there. And that's a good enough reason for me to make sure we do. "Look, Perkins, this is our—"

Another blast separates us, aimed to try and get us to turn around.

"This is our only chance, so come on!"

I make a run for it. I don't look back to see if Riley's coming with me.

A laser hits the doorknob right as I reach for it. I pull my hand back, but then, before Pete can fire again, I grab the knob. It's too hot, and for a second I think it's not going to turn, that it's *locked*.

Riley grabs my shoulder, pulling me out of the way of a blast to the head. I grab the knob again, and this time it turns.

We hurry through the door, shutting it behind us, and I don't think I've ever been this glad to see a flight of stairs.

CHAPTER 7

I t's windy and rainy and dark up on the roof. After running for my life, I was getting too hot, but now I pull my sleeves down over my hands.

It took me way too long to get up the stairs, even though there weren't that many of them. And maybe I wasn't too sorry to have a break between getting shot at and possibly fighting a ghost, but Riley being mad at me didn't make it any easier. It kept seeming like he was going to say something, only he didn't, and finally he stomped up to the landing at the top of the stairs to wait for me, like he didn't even want to be near me anymore.

And yeah, I probably deserved that, but it still sucked. Riley came here with me because he's my friend—because he *was*, anyway—and all he got for it was having that friendship thrown in his face. Not to mention that there's still a pretty big chance we're both going to end up dead.

"Well, Pete?!" I shout at the empty rooftop. "Show yourself!"

We stand there, waiting, but nothing happens. My eyes adjust a little to the darkness, but I don't see anything. Nothing besides the roof, anyway. And the housing for the stairwell we just came out of. The same one Pete had Kat tied to that night. I shudder and try to push away the memory, but my mind goes there anyway. Was this the spot I was standing in when Pete handed me that knife? When he wanted me to hurt her? And the ledge on the far side, behind us... That's where I jumped from.

"X," Riley says, his voice hard to hear over the wind, "are you okay?"

And over there is where Sarah pushed Pete. He fell off the roof, but he caught himself, and I was still under mind control. He was going to make me save him, and then he was going to kill us all. If my mom hadn't gotten here, if she hadn't stopped him...

"This is where it happened," I tell Riley. "Pete died here." *And no, I'm definitely not okay.* Besides reliving everything that happened that night, I feel like my feet are frozen in place, like if I take even one step in any direction, I'm going to go hurtling to my death. "Ghosts are supposed to return to the scene of the crime, right? So where is he?"

We're silent for a second. Cold rain whips my face and soaks into my hair and my sweatshirt.

"I don't think he's going to show," Riley says. "Maybe he can't."

"Come on." The rain speeds up and the wind howls right as I say that, drowning out my words.

"What?!" Riley shouts.

"Come on!" I motion for him to follow me back to the stairwell. My stomach twists up as soon as I decide to move, and suddenly I feel like I'm falling. I'm still on solid ground—I know that—but my body remembers what it was like to plummet through the air from up here. The way the pavement rushed up to meet me, and—

I flinch as Riley grabs my arm, bringing me out of it.

We make it to the stairwell. I lean against the wall once we're inside, keeping to the far side of the landing, and suck in my breath while Riley pushes the door shut. Cold water trickles down the back of my neck and under my shirt.

"What now?" Riley says.

I look around, double-checking that Pete can't see us. If there were lasers or speakers in here, Pete would have used them already, and I don't see any cameras.

I get out my phone.

Riley's eyebrows come together. "What are you doing?"

"Calling Sarah."

He glares at me.

"Maybe she can help." It's not like I'm calling her to have phone sex, which, judging by the look on his face, is what he must be assuming.

Sarah answers after a couple rings. She sounds a little out of breath. "Damien, this better be an emergency. I was in the middle of hanging up all the spider webs."

"It's, um, not an emergency," I lie.

"Then I'll— Wait, where are you? It sounds kind of echo-y. Where's Riley?"

"He's here. Look, Sarah, this isn't an emergency, but it's

really important. We need you to settle something for us."

"Whatever it is, we can talk about it later. At seven fifteen. I still have a bunch of stuff to do, so—"

"Sarah. Don't hang up." It's hard to convey how serious I am about that without also sounding like our lives are in danger. Which they are, of course, but I figure Sarah doesn't need to know that part. "Say there was a ghost. How would it, uh... How would it exist?"

"It wouldn't. Ghosts aren't real."

"I know, but *hypothetically*."

"If it was controlling an electrical system," Riley adds.

"Controlling an electrical system? Hmm." Sarah considers that. Then she says, "What's this for again?"

"Trivia night," I tell her.

"Aren't those usually at *bars*? You guys don't even have fake I.D.s like I told you to get. And how is this trivia?"

Riley holds out his hand for my phone. I hesitate, but I guess the trust thing works both ways. I hand it to him, and he puts it on speaker phone. "We're playing an RPG. A tabletop one. There's a ghost that's haunting Damien, and we're trying to figure out how to get rid of it."

"And it's controlling an electrical system?"

"Of an office building," I say.

"What rule system?"

"Reality," Riley says, wincing at how stupid that sounds.

Sarah's skeptical. "Reality? As in, real life?"

"Yep," I tell her. "It's one of those weird discount ones Zach got at that used book store."

"Well, in *reality* ghosts don't exist."

"Okay," Riley says, "but if one did? I mean, maybe someone who experienced a violent death or something?"

I can practically hear her rolling her eyes. "That's only on TV. There's no scientific basis for that to happen."

I take a deep breath. "But there *is* a ghost here. And he —it—died a violent death. And now it's messing with the electrical system of this building."

"You guys are taking this game *way* too seriously."

"But just, hypothetically, if that was the situation..."

Sarah's quiet for a few seconds. "Okay, maybe—and this is a really big maybe—if someone had a superpower like Pete's—"

"Whoa, Sarah. Who said anything about Pete?" I exchange a nervous glance with Riley.

"I did. It would make sense. Pete could broadcast signals, right? So if someone had a power like that and they were using it when they died, then *maybe* it would be possible for, like, an echo of them to be imprinted into the electrical system. Not in real life, of course, but hypothetically, for this weird game you're playing... it could work."

A tiny bit of relief washes over me, even though I still have no idea how we're getting out of this alive. "Great, Sarah. And how would we defeat it?"

"Well... If it's *in* the electrical system, you need to burn out the wiring."

"So, what? I can just zap a coffeemaker, and we're home free?"

"Zap?" Sarah says. "Are you playing *yourself*?"

"Kind of."

"The whole point of a role-playing game is to play a role."

"When you're already perfect, why change? And anyway, Riley's the one who still chose invisibility."

He smacks my arm.

"You guys have no imagination," Sarah says. "You're like when people go as themselves for Halloween."

"Uh-huh. So, we're sitting here playing this game as ourselves, and the rules of reality apply. How do I burn it out?"

"If it's in the whole building, then you need to burn out the whole building. But zapping it isn't going to work. You'd have to draw a bunch of power through a main line."

"Okay, that's— Wait, I can do that?"

She sighs. "It's your game, isn't it?"

"Yeah, but—"

"Oh, my God. Do you smell that?"

"Through the phone? No."

"My cookies! They're burnt! They were supposed to look like little ghosts with cute expressions, and now they look like they all died in a fire. And are really happy about it." Her voice fades a little as she shouts away from the phone. "Dad! You were supposed to be on cookie duty! Now is *not* the time to take a shower!" And then, back to us, "I have to go. I'll see you guys later."

"But, Sarah—"

She hangs up.

I slip my phone into my pocket. We should probably get going, now that we have some idea of how to stop

Pete. We should at least, like, discuss our plan. But neither of us says anything, or moves to leave, and Riley's got that look on his face like he's pissed at me and has something to say about it. His fists are clenched, and he opens his mouth, then closes it again, like he doesn't even know where to start.

"Let me make it easier for you, Perkins. I'm a selfish, manipulative bastard, just like Pete said, and you hate me and can't believe you were ever even friends with me. Does that about sum it up?"

"Why did it have to be her? Why did you have to try and sleep with *Sarah*?"

"Hey. That's *not* what happened."

"What did she even see in you? I mean, you're..."

"What? I'm what, Perkins?"

He gestures to me with one hand, as if that explains anything, and then lets it drop to his side. "I don't know, X. You're kind of a jerk. When I first met you, I didn't even get why Sarah was friends with you, let alone why she would have actually gone out with you. And now... I feel *so stupid*. You've made out with her. You didn't even care about her, but you two were going to sleep together."

"I never said I didn't care about her." The cold and damp that's soaked into my sweatshirt is starting to get to me. I wrap my arms around myself, but it just makes it worse.

"But you were *using* her. That's not caring about somebody." He looks at me like he doesn't even know who I am. Or maybe like he knows exactly who I am. Like he thinks he does, anyway.

"Yeah? Well, she was using me, too. And don't look at me like that, because you weren't there. I wanted to be her boyfriend, okay? I wanted to go out to dinner and hang out and stuff. But she didn't."

"Why? Because she just wanted to sleep with you?" He scoffs in disbelief.

"It wasn't like that. I think she liked me, too, but she wanted to treat it like an experiment, because…"

"Because she's Sarah," he says, sighing a little.

"It seemed safer that way. And I went along with it, because I liked her, and I thought she'd change her mind. About me not being her boyfriend. I'm not saying I was completely innocent, but I wasn't with her for that. I don't think she really was, either."

Riley makes a face and folds his arms. "Great. So you guys actually liked each other. If you hadn't realized you were in love with Kat, I never would have even met Sarah. Or you." He says it like that last part might not be such a bad thing.

"Don't be like that."

"Like *what*, X? Like I just found out that you and Sarah were going to sleep together? I know I wasn't going out with her then, and I know I hadn't even met you guys, but…" He covers his face with his hands. "It still hurts. She was going to lose her virginity with you. I thought that was something she'd only wanted to do with *me*. That us doing that together was… Don't laugh, okay?" He moves his hands away from his face so he can study mine. "I thought it was special. That it was something just between us."

"It *is*. Look, she didn't really want me. She saw the *X* on my thumb and thought I was some superhero."

He raises his eyebrows, like, *Aren't you?*

"And she…" I run my hands through my hair. They come back wet and cold. "You can't laugh about this, either, but she thought I looked like the Crimson Flash." Ugh. I cringe just saying it.

"But you do."

"Shut up."

"X, he's your *dad*. Of course you look like him."

"I don't, okay? I mean, yeah, maybe a teeny, tiny bit. We have the same hair color. And the same eyes. Big deal."

"And the same superpower."

"Minor details. I wouldn't go around saying I *look* like him."

"Even if you do."

I shrug. "My point is, Sarah thought I was somebody I wasn't. She didn't know me well enough to know she was getting someone like me instead of someone like you. And even if I hadn't figured out my feelings for Kat, it still wouldn't have worked with Sarah. She watches *The Crimson Flash and the Safety Kids* with a straight face."

He frowns at me, and I think he's going to argue that there's nothing wrong with that, but then he says something way worse. "How do I know I can even trust you, X? How do I know you're who I think you are?"

"How can you ask that? You *know* me."

"I thought I did, before tonight. But then I find out all this stuff about you, and now I don't know. You knew Pete for years. You two were way closer than we are, and you still did really horrible things to him. You guys were best friends, and if he couldn't trust you, then how am I supposed to?"

I hate that he's questioning that. My throat gets tight and my stomach feels like there's a rock in it. "It's different."

"Yeah, right."

"Me and Pete were never that close."

"But you knew him for years. We've only known each other for five months, and we've only not been trying to kill each other for two of them. If that. So..."

"We're friends, okay?"

"And I've seen how you treat your friends."

"No, you *haven't*."

Riley gives me an incredulous look.

"It's true. I might have known Pete for a long time, but that doesn't mean..." I take a deep breath. "I don't know if me and him were ever really friends."

"That doesn't make it okay. All the stuff you did."

"No, it doesn't." I glance over at him, then away again. "But you're not Pete. You can trust me."

"Why? Because you say so?" He shakes his head.

"Because... Because it's..." I hesitate, struggling to find the words. "I mean, I..."

"You know what, X? Forget it. Let's just go down there and get this over with. You can figure out whatever lie you were going to tell me later."

"No, just listen, okay? Maybe we've only been friends for a couple months. Maybe really only a few weeks. But we're…" I squeeze my eyes shut, then open them again. I hate that I actually have to say this. Especially since Riley's not exactly my biggest fan right now. "We're already better friends than me and Pete ever were."

"Yeah?" His eye meet mine, studying my face. Then he sighs, and his shoulders slump. "I just really wish I could believe that."

CHAPTER 8

We go downstairs, back to the top floor, where Pete's waiting for us.

"I knew you'd be back," he says. He doesn't fire any lasers yet, but he keeps them trained on us. "What did you think you were going to do? *Fly away?*" He laughs.

I hold up my hands. "I did what you wanted. I told the truth. Now let us go."

"And I told you, you're not calling the shots tonight. You tried to *leave.*"

The lasers charge up.

"You tried to kill us!" Riley shouts. "What were we supposed to do?"

"You were going to leave, but it's an awful long way down, isn't it? *I should know.*"

I swallow, remembering the fall and imagining what it would have been like if I hadn't saved myself. If I couldn't. "I didn't want you to fall, Pete." But I didn't want to die, either. "You have to know that."

"I don't have to do anything! But you. *You* have to do what I say!"

Several lasers fire at once. Me and Riley both drop to the floor, avoiding getting hit. Singe marks line the walls. We get up and start running.

"You can't talk your way out of this!" Pete screams. "You twist the truth and you lie and you manipulate everyone, until you've got them eating out of your hand, but *not me*. Not this time!"

A laser just misses me.

"X," Riley says, tilting his head toward an electrical outlet on the wall.

Lightning tingles in my hands, ready to zap it, but Sarah said that wouldn't work. I make it go away, but I'm not sure what I'm supposed to actually do. And trying to figure it out with lasers aimed at my head isn't making it any easier.

Riley shouts at the ceiling. "Like you haven't been twisting the truth and manipulating us this whole time! Yeah, Damien screwed up. Probably a lot. But you screwed up, too!"

All the lasers point at Riley. He's buying me more time to figure this out, and I can't afford to waste it.

"You weren't there," Pete says, sounding deadly serious. "And if you think he hasn't been doing the same things to you, then you're delusional."

I hold my hand up, toward the socket. I've never done this before, but Sarah seemed to think it was possible. Well, possible in the imaginary game we were playing. But it doesn't really matter, because either I can do this, or

Pete kills us. And I do *not* want that to be how I die, and I sure as hell don't want it to be how Riley does.

"Oh, yeah?" Riley makes a dismissive sound. "I know he's awful. I didn't need you to tell me that!"

Gee, thanks, Perkins. That's just what I need to hear while I'm trying to save our lives.

I can't feel the electricity in the wall, but I crank mine up and imagine drawing more of it toward me.

"I saw your face," Pete says. "I saw how horrified you were when you found out some of the crap he's pulled. Don't tell me you already knew!"

"He broke my finger! He fought with me, he did everything he could to get me out of Sarah's life. He's lied to me. He's tried to manipulate me."

Tried to?

"And he's selfish, like you said. I knew all that before I ever stepped foot in here."

Electricity from the socket flows from it over to me. It's working. I try pulling harder, because something needs to happen, and it needs to happen now. Because Riley's diversion can't last much longer, and, to be honest, I'm not sure I want to hear any more of it.

"But that's only one side of him, because he's also—"

"Hey!" Pete shouts. "What are you doing?!"

A laser fires at me, but I manage to dodge out of the way without breaking my connection with the wall socket. I focus on making it hurry up, and then suddenly the electricity stops. The wiring must have burnt out, just like Sarah said. There's about half a second where I feel this huge wave of relief, because *I did it*, Pete's finally gone.

And then another laser almost hits me.

"What the hell was that?!" Pete screams. "Did you think you could hurt me?!"

More lasers fire, and we take off down the hall again.

"It didn't work!" I tell Riley. Not like he didn't know.

"Sarah said it has to be a main line!"

"And that wasn't?"

A laser nearly blasts him, but I push him into the wall, out of the way. He glares at me, like I did it for fun or something.

"We need something that has more power," he says.

"What else has more power?" I duck out of the way as a laser hits the wall, leaving a singe mark. And then I know what I have to do.

Riley grabs my arm. "No, X!"

"Do you want to die tonight?!"

"If you draw more power through the lasers, they'll—"

"I know!" They'll be more powerful. Pete already cranked them up, and if I do this, they're going to be deadly. But what choice do I have? "Just don't get hit."

"*You're* going to get hit! He knows what you're trying to—"

"Look, I get it if you don't want to be friends with me. After everything I've done, and after all that stuff you said, I don't even know why you ever were."

"X, I didn't—"

"I know you don't trust me! But you have to trust me on this." Because it's our only hope. Because I don't know what else to do.

I hold my hands up and draw power from a laser on the

ceiling.

It twitches, repositioning itself to point right at my heart. Or maybe I should say *Pete* repositions it.

"Back off, Damien," he says. "You're ruining this for me. I wanted to watch you try and get down all those stairs. But don't think I won't shoot you."

I pull harder. Sweat prickles on my forehead and down my back.

Pete fires one of the lasers at the wall, and it does way more than just singe it this time—it blasts a chunk out of it.

"If you shoot me, Pete, then you're just as bad as I am. Because I got you killed, right? You were only in that situation, trying to murder me and my friends, because of what *I* did to you."

"Shut up! You don't get another warning shot!"

But if he was going to kill me, maybe he would have done it already. Maybe. "This whole thing tonight is about how you're so much better than me, right? So if you kill me—"

"Man, I'll still be better than you, because at least I'll have done it myself!"

Pete fires a laser. And it's not a warning shot, but it's not aimed at me, either.

It's aimed at Riley.

I move without thinking, because I don't need to. There's no question of what I'm going to do. I break the connection with the electricity, making my lightning die down, and I lunge at Riley. I push him out of the way right as the laser hits.

It feels like a hot knife slices into my shoulder. It just barely hits me, and it hurts like hell, but it doesn't blow me up. I'm still in one piece. And so is Riley.

"X! Watch out!"

I twist out of the way of another blast. I hold up my hand to finish this. "You're not going to kill me, Pete! And you're not going to kill anyone I care about!"

"You think you can hurt me?!" Pete screams. "You think you can come in here and just—"

"Yeah, I can," I say, right as I draw one last surge of electricity out of the laser.

The lights go off. Everything powers down. And then Pete *finally* shuts the hell up.

X·X·X

Riley takes the stairs down.

I take the elevator shaft.

Which is pretty much the last thing I want to do tonight, especially after everything we've been through. But my only other options were taking the stairs, which wasn't going to happen, or trying to fly off the roof in the wind and the rain, which was really, *really* not going to happen.

Flying very slowly down the dark, creepy elevator shaft, with only a flashlight app on my phone for company, is pretty terrifying, and not something I ever want to do again. It's only *slightly* less terrifying than being dropped in an elevator that Pete was controlling. Either way, I think I've had enough terror for one Halloween.

And pretty much the rest of my life.

I meet up with Riley on the second floor, and he turns invisible and scouts ahead to make sure we avoid any police, who are trying to figure out what the hell's going on. We stop at the security room on the way out, and I zap all the computers, destroying any footage of us. A lot of stuff was burnt out anyway, so it shouldn't be too suspicious.

By the time we make it back to Riley's car, it feels like a week has gone by, but according to his clock, we only got here a little over an hour ago. We still have almost thirty minutes to make it to Sarah's.

I climb into the passenger seat, while Riley gets in the driver's side. He turns on the car but doesn't move. Rain pounds on the roof and on the windshield, and even though I'm kind of soaked from walking the two blocks over here, it feels good to be somewhere dry.

"Perkins. Let's just—"

"About what I said in there."

"Don't tell me you didn't mean it, because you did."

"Yeah, I did."

"Oh." I swallow. I mean, I knew that, but I still expected him to try and apologize or something. "Okay. Great. At least I know where I stand."

"No, you don't. Pete didn't let me finish. What I was going to say was that you are all of those things, but you're also loyal, and brave, and you'd do anything for the people you care about."

"But you don't trust me."

"I... You risked your life for me, X."

"It just got my shoulder. I've had worse."

He shakes his head. "You didn't know it wasn't going to kill you. It *could have* killed you, if it had hit in the wrong place."

"Just because you can trust me to save your life doesn't mean you can trust me in general."

"I was trying to say all that *before* you saved my life." Riley flips on the windshield wipers, but he still doesn't start driving. "I shouldn't have let Pete get to me."

"I did all those things to him, though. I mean, I didn't steal Kat. But I knew he liked her—I just didn't care."

"That was the past. It was between you and him. You've never been anything but trustworthy to me."

I raise an eyebrow at him.

"Since we've been friends, that is. I couldn't picture you telling Pete about hearing a ghost."

"Nope. And if I had, there's no way he would have gone with me to check it out." And he especially wouldn't have been the one to suggest it.

"So, I believe you. About things being different. Maybe Pete couldn't trust you, but you obviously couldn't trust him, either. You can trust me."

"Okay, but I get it if you don't—"

"I'm your friend. I want to be, I mean. If you still...?"

"Yeah, of course I do, Perkins. But after everything you found out tonight..." I sigh. "I don't get why you'd still want to hang out with me."

"Because I like you, X."

I wait for him to say something more complicated than that, but he doesn't. "That's it?"

He shrugs. "People are more than just a list of all the bad things they've done. We've been through a lot together, and I'd like to think that counts for something."

"It does. But... you're not mad?"

"Well." He lets out a deep breath. "I wouldn't say that. But who you were with Pete... It's not who you are now. It's not who you are with *me*. So maybe I'm still upset about some things, but the truth is, you're my friend, and nothing that happened tonight is going to change that."

CHAPTER 9

W hen we get to Sarah's house, it's obvious we're the first to arrive for her party. There are no extra cars out front, and Sarah answers the door before we even get a chance to knock. Though that might have more to do with Heraldo, her Great Dane, barking at us from the backyard than it does Sarah not having anything to do.

I check my phone, just in case we got here too early, but it's 7:16.

"You're late," Sarah says, standing aside so we can come in.

"*Fashionably* late," I correct her.

"One minute doesn't count as fashionable."

"Wow," Riley says, surveying all the decorations. "This looks great."

No wonder it took her so long to get everything ready. Fake spiderwebs stretch across the walls, along with some orange and black streamers. The dining table is covered in food. There are little bowls of candy, plus Sarah's burnt ghost cookies, gingerbread zombies, a plastic bucket of chocolate dirt with gummy worms in it, and a couple dozen cupcakes that have been decorated to look like pumpkins and spiders and stuff. Some of them look better than others, but they're all pretty detailed and must have taken a lot of work.

It looks like she's expecting a bunch of people to show up, which is kind of a relief, because that means I won't have to be alone with just her and Riley. Not that the three of us don't hang out a lot, but... Well, that was before Riley found out me and Sarah were maybe going to sleep together.

Riley takes his coat off and hangs it on a hook on the wall. My sweatshirt's pretty damp, but I leave it on, because my shoulder was bleeding earlier, and I don't need Sarah asking questions. I head over to the dining table and pick up a cupcake that looks like a spider. "Don't worry, Sarah," I say as I stuff half of it into my mouth. "I made sure to take the worst one. Its eyes were crooked."

She folds her arms. "It doesn't matter. Patty from the retirement home called ten minutes ago. Their van broke down today and is still in the shop, so none of them are coming. It's just us."

"Wait." I swallow down a bite of cupcake. "Are you telling me that everyone else you invited was from the *retirement home*?" Sarah's been volunteering at a retirement home for supervillains as part of her self-appointed rehabilitation.

"I'm making lots of new friends, and I thought it would

be fun to invite them over."

"You didn't invite anyone else, like, our age?"

"I tried, but Kat didn't answer my email. And Dad went to a work party."

"Yeah, he's not exactly our age, either."

Riley puts an arm around her. "I'm sorry no one showed up."

"At least you guys are here. And maybe it's a good thing the van broke down, because there's been a lot of drama brewing between Agnes and Sheila, because they both like Andrew. And I wasn't sure if I should invite all of them, but I didn't want to leave anyone out or choose sides, either. But the three of us can still hang out. I have some Halloween movies on my computer."

Watching movies on her computer sounds kind of intimate, and like it might actually be code for "let's make Damien feel like a third wheel." And *normally* I wouldn't care—I wouldn't let them get rid of me so easily—but after everything that's happened tonight, it just feels wrong.

As if to prove my point about it seeming intimate, Riley kisses Sarah. It's the kind of kiss where he puts his arms around her, and she leans into him, and it's like they suddenly have no idea I'm here.

Which I think is my cue to leave. "Everything looks great, Sarah, but I'm going to go."

She steps back from Riley. "You just got here. And it's raining really hard."

"I was really only in it for the old people, and now that they're not coming, I just don't see the point."

Riley's eyebrows come together. "X, come on."

I hold up my phone. "I just got a text from Kat. She wants me to come over."

Sarah squints at me. "On a school night?"

I roll my eyes at her. "I'm just... You guys watch the movie, okay? I'll go."

Sarah looks like she's about to say something to that, but then Heraldo scratches at the back door, and she goes to let him in.

Which is *definitely* my cue to leave.

"X, wait," Riley says. "You don't have to do this."

"Yeah, I do. You guys can have the house to yourselves and 'watch movies' on her bed. You *really* don't need me here for that."

Riley's face turns red. He glances over toward the back door, like he's afraid Sarah might have heard, then back at me. "We're not doing that."

"But you might. If I wasn't here. So I'll just get out of your way—problem solved."

He sighs. "After everything that happened earlier, you seriously think I'm going to... Look, it's not happening right now. And even if it was, I don't want things to be weird between us."

"That's why I'm getting out of your way."

"No, I mean, I don't want you to do that. You never would have had to run off like this before tonight, so don't do it now."

"But—"

"We're all friends. You don't have to run away from your friends."

Heraldo comes bounding into the living room, soaking wet and covered in mud. He runs straight over and jumps up on me, knocking me back a step and getting pawprints all over my sweatshirt.

"Heraldo!" Sarah scolds. *"Down."*

He gets down, then shakes himself off, spraying me with cold water.

"Ugh." I wipe droplets off my face with my sleeve.

"Damien was just telling me that he's *staying*," Riley says.

Sarah brightens at that. "You are? What about Kat? Is she coming over?"

"Uh, no. But I got another text, and... I guess I can stay."

Heraldo pushes his nose into Riley's hand, though of course his giant tail smacks my leg as he wags it back and forth. Then he barks and takes off for the front door, right before there's a knock.

"Stay," Sarah tells him. Once he's behaving himself, she opens the door.

"Hi, Sarah," Zach says.

Amelia pushes past both of them, not waiting for an invitation. "It's so cold out there!" she says, wrapping her arms around herself. Both her and Zach are wet from the rain and, well, *bedraggled* is the word that really comes to mind. Amelia's hair hangs in soggy clumps. She's wearing her coat, but she's obviously wearing the ugly bridesmaid's dress underneath. She must have changed after we left. There are patches of white and gray face paint on her cheeks and forehead, but it looks like it's mostly coming off, and her mascara's running like crazy.

Zach has similar patches of face paint, and it looks like he sprayed his hair silver again, but it's partly washed out from the rain. He's not wearing his Brogdon the Third costume with the extra tentacle arms—just a Halloween themed T-shirt and jeans.

"So," I say, "I assume you guys won best costume."

Amelia's mouth turns down, like she just ate something sour. "Shut up."

"The party sucked," Zach says.

Amelia squeaks in outrage. "It didn't!"

Zach gives her a look.

Her shoulders slump. "Okay, it totally sucked. We went as a zombie Prom couple."

I raise my eyebrows at Zach's jeans and T-shirt. "That's what you're wearing to Prom?"

"Mom would kill me if I got paint on my nice clothes."

"And *you* wore your bathing suit to Homecoming," Amelia says to me, "so I wouldn't talk if I were you."

"Tell me you at least won cutest couple."

She punches me in the shoulder.

White-hot pain erupts where that laser sliced into me earlier. I gasp and try really hard not to look like I'm in agony, which, judging by the way everyone's staring at me, I'm totally failing at.

"Are you okay?" Zach asks.

"I'm fine. Amelia just doesn't know her own strength."

"Whatever," Amelia says, taking off her coat. "I've had the *worst* night—you don't even know. So don't make fun of me."

She's had the worst night? Me and Riley exchange a glance.

"Nobody could tell what our costumes were supposed to be. And I overheard some girl—who Kim didn't even invite; she just tagged along with a friend—saying that we should win *worst* costume, and someone else actually *laughed*. Even though it wasn't funny."

"You weren't exactly invited to *this* party," I tell her.

"But Riley was, and Zach's his brother, and I'm Zach's girlfriend."

"Uh, *I* was invited, and I'm your brother."

"I'm not tagging along with my *brother*." She shakes her head, like that would be ridiculous.

"Right."

"We were just about to watch a movie," Sarah says. "I guess if it's all of us, I should hook it up to the TV."

She has to order Heraldo off the couch twice as everyone takes their shoes off and settles in to watch. Everyone except me, anyway. I step into the kitchen and get out my phone to call Kat.

It rings for a while, but I don't hang up. I feel this huge wave of relief when she answers. "Damien?"

There's music playing in the background, and I can hear people laughing and talking. "Is this a bad time?"

"I was bobbing for apples, and I couldn't hear my phone. I *hate* that game, by the way."

I laugh. "I didn't think people really played that."

Riley pokes his head into the kitchen. "We're about to start the movie."

"I'll be there in a minute."

He nods and ducks back out.

"You want to tell me what's up?" Kat says. "Because you sound kind of weird, and you're obviously in the middle of something."

"I just wanted to tell you happy Halloween."

"And?" she says, sounding skeptical.

She knows me way too well. My throat gets tight, and I swallow. "And that I love you."

Silence. And then, sounding kind of freaked out, "Damien, are you okay? Did something happen?"

"No. I mean, I'm okay." Mostly. "Nothing happened. I was just thinking about all that crap with Pete—"

"Oh."

"—and I just wanted you to know that. That I love you."

"I love you, too. You know *that*, right?"

"Yeah." I suck in a deep breath, and I keep my voice low. "I did some awful things to Pete. I've just been thinking about it. About how I treated him."

"It wasn't your fault, what happened that night. That was all him."

But maybe Pete was right about me having a hand in it. "I wasn't a good friend. Neither was he, but… it's not an excuse."

She's quiet for a second. For a really long, agonizing second. "We've all made mistakes. I was horrible to you." She whispers it, too ashamed to say it out loud.

"It's in the past. It's not who you are now."

"The things you did to Pete, the way you guys treated each other, that's in the past, too. It's not your fault he's dead."

"I know." At least, I mostly do. Some days it still feels like my fault. Especially today.

"You're a good boyfriend, Damien. And a good friend. To me, to Riley, to Zach, and… even to Sarah." I can hear her making a face at that. "Pete's gone—you can't fix things with him. But you can be there for everyone who's still here."

I close my eyes, thinking that over. I run a hand through my hair. "I wish you were here. Or that I was there."

"Come over this weekend." It's not a question.

"I'll be there."

Someone shouts something at her in the background—something about it being her turn to pin the stem on the pumpkin or something—and she tells me she has to go. We say our good-byes and hang up.

Everyone's waiting for me in the living room. Amelia's in the armchair, and Zach's sitting on the floor in front of her, with Heraldo pretty much lying on top of him. Sarah and Riley are on the couch. Sarah's on the far side, with her laptop, and Riley's sitting in the middle. He's obviously saved a spot for me, and he jerks his head toward the free space next to him when I come in.

"It's about time," Amelia whines. "Just because you and Kat are having drama doesn't mean the rest of us should have to suffer."

I put a hand to my chest as I sit down on the couch. "Thank you, Amelia, for enduring the hardship of having to wait two minutes for me. It's brave men and women like you who make this country great."

She looks away. "Shut up."

"I've got three movies on here," Sarah says. "Do you want kind of scary, Japanese horror, or cheesy?"

"*Cheesy*," me and Riley both say at the same time.

"Yeah." Amelia sounds relieved. "Anything but Japanese horror."

"Aw, man," Zach says.

"We can get to that next," Sarah tells him. She fiddles with her laptop, getting the movie set up.

"Uh, Sarah?" I lean forward and tilt my head at her. "Two movies on a school night? Let's reign it in."

She ignores me. "Here we go. I think you said this one was your favorite, right?" She says that part to Riley.

The movie starts up on the TV. It's the same one we were watching earlier at his house—*I Know How You Killed Me*.

Riley freezes next to me.

I feel like I can't breathe.

"Oh!" Zach sounds really excited about it. "I love this one!"

Amelia grins at him. "Me, too."

"We watched this already," Riley says.

Amelia scowls. "Only part of it. And me and Zach haven't watched it together."

Zach shoots his brother a concerned look. "Come on, Riley. It's not Halloween without it."

"It is this year," I tell him.

"We shouldn't have to miss out just because *Damien* hates it." Amelia folds her arms across her chest and rolls her eyes at me.

"How can you hate this movie?" Zach asks. "It's so awesome."

"What can I say? I have no taste."

"His friend died," Amelia fake whispers, really loudly, to Zach. "He's super traumatized. He can't even talk about it."

Zach and Sarah's eyes both dart over to me, while Riley makes a point of looking anywhere else.

"Do you have anything that's about an amazing brother killing his really horrible sister?" I ask through clenched teeth. "Because I should probably watch it *before* it happens in real life."

They're still staring at me. Sarah pauses the movie.

"I'm *fine*, okay? But I am changing my vote to Japanese horror."

Riley nods. "Me, too."

"*Yes*," Zach says.

Sarah shrugs. "Okay. If that's what you want."

"Unless it's about a ghost," I add.

She raises her eyebrows at me. "It's Japanese horror, Damien. Of course it's about a ghost."

Great. "What's the third option?"

"*Sleeping Zomb-beauty*. It's a retelling of Sleeping Beauty, except when everyone in her castle wakes up, they're flesh-eating zombies. She's the only one who's not, but it turns out the prince who woke her up was a werewolf, and now she is, too, and she's the only one who can save everyone. But she has to fight her way out of the castle first."

"He kissed her, and now she's a werewolf? Or he actually bit her? You know what? It so doesn't matter. *This* is the one."

"*Uh!*" Amelia screeches. "No way! That one looked so stupid. And it doesn't even make sense to be called that if she's not a zombie."

"It's supposed to have a lot of sex, violence, and unrealistic action scenes," Sarah adds.

I point a finger at Amelia. "You weren't even invited to this party. You don't get a vote." I nudge Riley with my elbow. "Back me up on this, Perkins."

His eyes go wide, like he didn't expect to be dragged into the middle of this. "I don't... I'm not saying anyone doesn't get a vote. But I *do* want to watch this movie."

"Zach does, too. Right, Zach?"

Amelia scowls. "If I don't get a vote, he shouldn't get one, either!"

"Let's watch it," Zach says.

"Okay." Sarah nods and pokes at her computer. "*Sleeping Zomb-beauty* it is."

"I hate you." Amelia glares at me. "And this is *so* the worst night ever."

"Maybe for you," I tell her. And yeah, Pete's ghost dredging up all that stuff from the past and trying to kill us was definitely a low point. But he's gone, and I'm here, surrounded by my friends. Kat loves me. Riley still wants to hang out with me, despite all the reasons he shouldn't. Sarah didn't want me to leave, Zach thinks I'm great, and there are a couple dozen cupcakes on the table that are all up for grabs. And despite what she said, I know Amelia doesn't really hate me.

So maybe for her it's the worst night ever. But for me?

It's definitely looking up.

ACKNOWLEDGMENTS

This story started out as part of the kickstarter for *The Betrayal of Renegade X*. For one of the stretch goals, I said I'd write the Renegade X holiday special, and backers would get to vote on which holiday I wrote about.

I was picturing something cheesy and light-hearted—a short story that was only 10–20 pages. Even when the votes were overwhelmingly in favor of Halloween, and I knew I wouldn't be writing, like, Damien saves Christmas or anything, I still thought it would be short and light. I had no idea it would turn into a super-intense, 100-page novella. But I'm glad that it did.

So, a huge thanks goes out to all the kickstarter backers, because without you guys, this story wouldn't exist.

Thanks also go out to Chloë Tisdale, who, as always, discussed every aspect of this story endlessly with me.

And thanks to all the fans who love these books and keep asking for more. Your support means the world.

ABOUT THE AUTHOR

CHELSEA M. CAMPBELL grew up in the Pacific Northwest, where it rains a lot. And then rains some more. She finished her first novel when she was twelve, sent it out, and promptly got rejected. Since then, she's earned a degree in Latin and Ancient Greek, become an obsessive knitter and fiber artist, and started a collection of glass grapes.

Besides writing, studying ancient languages, and collecting useless objects, Chelsea is a pop-culture fangirl at heart and can often be found rewatching episodes of *Buffy the Vampire Slayer, Parks and Recreation,* or dying a lot in *Dark Souls.* You can visit her online at www.chelseamcampbell.com.